STICKER DRESSING
KNIGHTS

Illustrated by Jean-Sébastien Deheeger

Written by Kate Davies

Designed by Emily Bornoff

Additional design by Lisa Verrall

CONTENTS

You'll find all the sticker pages in the middle of the book.

Historical consultants: Robert Smith and Fahmida Suleman

NORMANS AND SAXONS

It's the year 1066, and knights from Normandy, in France, have just invaded England. They're battling the Saxon knights who live there. All the knights wear pointy helmets and tough chain mail shirts called hauberks. They fight with heavy swords and protect themselves with painted wooden shields.

David (Norman knight)   Edgar (Saxon knight)

Laurent (Norman knight)

3

THE CRUSADES

These knights have come all the way from Europe to the Middle East to battle Arab warriors in a war called a Crusade. They want to seize control of Jerusalem, a holy city. The knights wear chain mail from head to toe, with long cloaks over the top. They have thick leather gloves and metal helmets. King Richard's helmet has a crown on top, to show he's the king.

Sir Geoffrey

Sir Bernard

King Richard I of England

ARAB WARRIORS

In a camp in the sandy desert, Arab warriors are resting after battling with European knights. They wear chain mail, like their enemies, but they fight with curved swords instead of straight ones. Some of the warriors wear headscarves called turbans.

Saladin

Ishaq

Uthman

FIGHTING IN FRANCE

It's 1346, and French and English knights are fighting over who should be king in France. The knights wear armour plates on top of their chain mail to protect their arms and legs. Their shields are decorated with colourful patterns known as coats of arms, which show the other knights who they are.

English knight   Prince Edward of England

French knight

CASTLE SIEGE

These knights are attacking one of their enemies' castles, to try to take it over. All the knights wear heavy suits of shiny metal armour, with padded jackets underneath, to protect every part of their bodies. Their breast plates have ridges on them, so arrows will bounce off.

Sir Jacob

Sir Nicholas

Sir Charles

Armour for horses

Sometimes even horses wear armour, so they don't get hurt when they ride into battle. The metal plates on their necks are designed so they can move around easily.

Lancelot

Caspian

NORMANS AND SAXONS

Follow the numbers and arrows to add the stickers in the right order.

① David's sabatons (metal shoes)

① Edgar's greaves (leather leg protection)

② Chain mail hauberk

③ Chain mail ventail

③ Ventail (face protection)

④ Helmet with a nose guard

⑤ Shield

② Chain mail hauberk

① Laurent's greaves (leather leg protection)

④ Helmet with a nose guard

⑤ Shield

④ Helmet with a nose guard

⑥ Sword

⑤ Shield

② Chain mail hauberk

③ Helmet with a nose guard

④ Axe

⑥ Sword

THE CRUSADES

Follow the numbers and arrows to add the stickers in the right order.

1 Sir Geoffrey's helmet with a nose guard

2 Metal shoes (sabatons)

1 Sir Bernard's metal helmet

2 Metal shoes (sabatons)

1 King Richard's chain mail ventail (face protection) with a helmet and crown on top

2 Metal shoes (sabatons)

3 Brown wool surcoat with cloak on top

3 Chain mail with white surcoat and wool cloak on top

3 Chain mail with white surcoat and wool cloak on top

Sword

Long shield

Long shield with metal studs

Mace (wooden club with metal spikes)

Sword

ARAB WARRIORS

Follow the numbers and arrows to add the stickers in the right order.

① Ishaq's chain mail with a metal breast plate on top

Pointed helmet with chain mail underneath to protect his neck.

② ③ Spear

① Saladin's chain mail with wrist guards and a linen tunic on top

② Helmet and turban

③ Boots

④ Shield

⑤ Sword

① Uthman's chain mail with linen shirt over the top

② Turban

③ Shield

④ Sword

⑤ Boots

FIGHTING IN FRANCE

Follow the numbers and arrows to add the stickers in the right order.

① Prince Edward's suit of armour, with linen surcoat

② Helmet with ventail (face protection) and crown to show he's a prince

③ Shield showing his coat of arms

④ Sword

① English knight's shield

② Sword

PAGES 8-9

CASTLE SIEGE

Follow the numbers and arrows to add the stickers in the right order.

① Sir Nicholas's helmet

① Sir Jacob's helmet

① Sir Charles's suit of armour, surcoat and leather belt

② Shield

② Shield

③ Sword

③ Sword

④ Sword with carved hilt (grip)

② Helmet with ventail underneath, and carved hinges to hold his armour together

③ Shield

PAGES 10-11

ARMOUR FOR HORSES

Follow the numbers and arrows to add
the stickers in the right order.

① Caspian's crupper – metal plates to protect his back

③ Crinet (neck armour) and shaffron to protect his face

Peytral (chest armour)

② Leather saddle on cloth blanket, so it doesn't rub

① Lancelot's golden crinet and shaffron

② Leather saddle on a cloth blanket

③ Crupper to protect his back

COATS OF ARMS   Put the stickers anywhere you like on the shields and flags, to make different coats of arms.

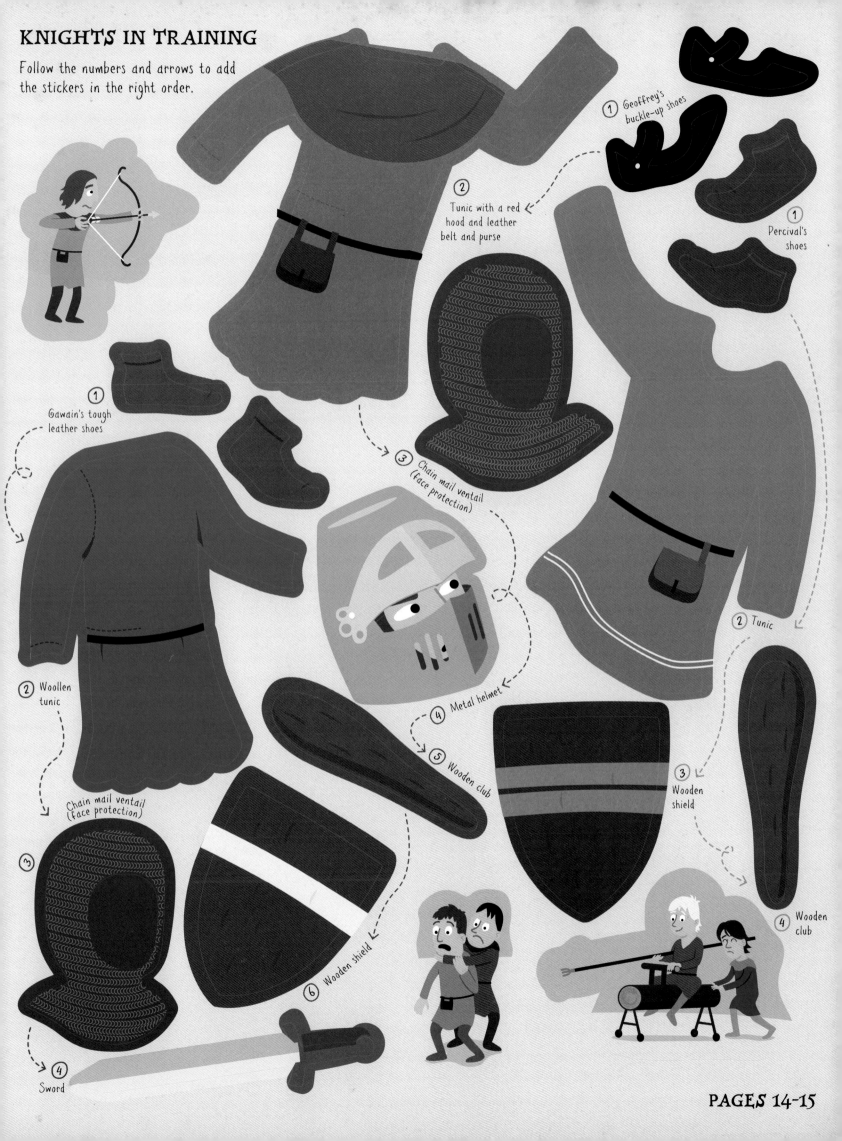

KNIGHTS IN TRAINING

Follow the numbers and arrows to add the stickers in the right order.

① Geoffrey's buckle-up shoes

② Tunic with a red hood and leather belt and purse

① Percival's shoes

① Gawain's tough leather shoes

③ Chain mail ventail (face protection)

② Tunic

④ Metal helmet

② Woollen tunic

⑤ Wooden club

③ Wooden shield

③ Chain mail ventail (face protection)

④ Wooden club

④ Sword

⑥ Wooden shield

THE TOURNAMENT

Follow the numbers and arrows to add the stickers in the right order.

① Sir Colgrevance's metal shoes, called sabatons

Suit of armour with surcoat on top

① Sir Agrevaine's suit of armour with surcoat on top

② Metal shoes, called sabatons

④ Jousting helmet with a unicorn on top

③ Tough leather gloves

③ Tough leather gloves

④ Long wooden lance

⑤ Long wooden lance

⑤ Jousting helmet with a dragon on top

Guinevere's colourful cloth caparison (coat) with chain mail underneath

HUNTING AND HAWKING

Follow the numbers and arrows to add the stickers in the right order.

Hawks

Crossbow

① Sir Tristram's hat

② Doublet (jacket) and hunting horn

① Sir Percy's hat

② Wool tunic and leather purse

① Sir Hector's wool tunic

② Hood

Leather shoes

③

④ Hunting knife

③

Leather shoes

Spear

Deer

③ Leather shoes

④ Hawk sitting on a leather glove

FANTASTIC FEAST

Follow the numbers and arrows to add the stickers in the right order.

① Sir Geoffrey's woollen hose (stockings)

Cedric's doublet and leather belt

①

② Sturdy leather boots

Feste's woollen hose and shoes with curly toes

①

② Hat with jingling bells on it

③ Wooden stick for the jester to twirl

④ Multi-coloured tunic with a red hood on top

② Fancy button-up doublet with gold embroidery

③ Leather shoes

Water jug

Goblet of wine

Plate of fish

THE GRAND FESTIVAL
Follow the numbers and arrows to add the stickers in the right order.

① Duke of Buckingham's breast plate

② Metal plate armour to protect his arms and hands

① King Henry's breast plate

② Metal plate armour to protect his arms and hands

① King Francis's breast plate

② Metal plate armour to protect his arms and hands

③ Helmet

③ Helmet

③ Helmet

PAGES 22-23

ARISE, SIR KNIGHT

Follow the numbers and arrows to add the stickers in the right order.

② Sword belt and scabbard to hold his sword

① Sir Galahad's surcoat and leather belt

③ Sword

PAGE 24

COATS OF ARMS

Every knight has his own coat of arms – patterns or pictures on his shield, so everyone knows who he is. Use the stickers to design lots of different ones.

13

KNIGHTS IN TRAINING

Young knights-in-training, known as squires, are practising their
fighting skills in a castle courtyard. They wear woollen tunics which
won't tear easily. One boy practises using his heavy sword, while
his friends battle with wooden clubs and shields.

Gawain

Geoffrey

Percival

THE TOURNAMENT

Sir Colgrevance and Sir Agrevaine are about to take part in a jousting contest called a tournament. Jousters try to knock each other off their horses with long lances. Their helmets hide their faces, but they wear their coats of arms proudly. Even the horses wear their masters' coats of arms.

Guinevere

Sir Colgrevance   Sir Agrevaine

HUNTING AND HAWKING

These knights are hunting outside the king's castle. They wear comfortable clothes, and hunt with spears and bows and arrows. Sir Tristram carries a horn, which he blows to let his friends know when he's found a deer to chase. Sir Hector is using a hawk to catch small animals. His thick leather gloves protect his hands from the hawk's sharp claws.

Sir Tristram

Sir Percy

Sir Hector

FANTASTIC FEAST

After a long day's hunting, knights and their ladies are having a grand feast in the castle. Sir Geoffrey is wearing his finest clothes. The jester wears a colourful costume and a silly hat, and makes everyone laugh. The serving boy wears a simple coat and sturdy boots.

Sir Geoffrey

Feste the jester

Cedric the serving boy

THE GRAND FESTIVAL

It's 1520, and the French king and the English king are holding a festival to celebrate their friendship. They both wear their fanciest suits of armour, decorated with gold to show off how rich and important they are. All the knights wear padded caps so their helmets don't hurt their heads.

Duke of Buckingham

King Henry VIII of England   King Francis I of France

ARISE, SIR KNIGHT

Sir Galahad has just been made a knight.
The king has given him his very own sword
and spiky spurs to wear on his heels, to
make his horse gallop faster.

Sir Galahad

First published in 2010 by Usborne Publishing Ltd., 83-85
Saffron Hill, London, EC1N 8RT, England. www.usborne.com.
Copyright ©, 2010 Usborne Publishing Ltd. The name Usborne
and the devices ♀⊕ are Trade Marks of Usborne Publishing Ltd.